E.W. Hutter

Female Education

Anatiposi

E.W. Hutter

Female Education

Reprint of the original, first published in 1859.

1st Edition 2023 | ISBN: 978-3-38231-202-2

Anatiposi Verlag is an imprint of Outlook Verlagsgesellschaft mbH.

Verlag (Publisher): Outlook Verlag GmbH, Zeilweg 44, 60439 Frankfurt, Deutschland
Vertretungsberechtigt (Authorized to represent): E. Roepke, Zeilweg 44, 60439 Frankfurt, Deutschland
Druck (Print): Books on Demand GmbH, In de Tarpen 42, 22848 Norderstedt, Deutschland

FEMALE EDUCATION:

ITS IMPORTANCE—THE HELPS AND THE HINDRANCES.

ADDRESS,

DELIVERED BEFORE THE FACULTY AND STUDENTS OF THE

Susquehanna Female College,

AT

SELINSGROVE, PA.

On Tuesday Evening, November 8th, 1859,

BY

REV. E. W. HUTTER,

PASTOR OF ST. MATTHEW'S LUTHERAN CHURCH,

PHILADELPHIA.

BALTIMORE:
PUBLISHED BY T. NEWTON KURTZ,
151 WEST PRATT STREET.
1859.

REV. E. W. HUTTER'S ADDRESS.

Ladies and Gentlemen:

Without controversy, one of the profoundest topics that can possibly challenge human investigation, is, THE MORAL, INTELLECTUAL, AND SOCIAL ELEVATION OF WOMAN. Accordingly, the various modes in which women have been treated, in all ages and countries of the world, from the days of the patriarchs down to the present period, constitute a research, always instructive and profitable, and not unfrequently curious and melancholy. The history of woman, indeed, is the history of the world, for not more certainly, nor more immediately, are the ebb and flow of the tides connected with lunar influences, than are the proper and rational estimate and appreciation of woman identified with the advancement and deterioration of nations—not in the arts and sciences—but in the refinement of popular manners—in the progress of civilization—in the emancipation of the understanding from pernicious prejudices—and in the recognition and establishment of principles and theories indissolubly interwoven with the welfare of the human family.

The recorded annals of the past disclose, with melancholy clearness, the fact, that woman has never yet had assigned to her that rank in the scale of civilization and refinement for which the beneficent Creator in the beginning graciously designed her. Some one has said, in language of marked poetic beauty, that woman was not originally taken from man's *head*, to be his lord and master—nor from his *feet*, to be his tool and slave—but from under his arm, that she might be always sure of his protection,—from his side, to symbolize equality and companionship—from near his heart, that she might ever love and be beloved! But, alas, how sadly has sinful and rebellious man thwarted the beneficent designs of Heaven! In most ages and countries woman has served as a mere "hewer of wood and drawer of water" to her professed superior. Of this fact, the unbroken succession of history furnishes irrefragable authentications. In Sparta the women were brutalized by the very laws that should have served for their elevation. The Athenians, in their palmiest state of learning and literature, condemned their females to ignorance and obscurity. Cultivation *then* was a luxury only to be acquired by the forfeiture of reputation, for, whilst a courtesan might be entombed among warriors and statesmen, and have her name enshrined in the same temples, the virtuous wives and daughters of those same heroes never could rise above the distaff and the spindle. The Romans, though excessively austere, treated their women better than their more romantic and imaginative neighbors, the Greeks, for, if they were a less refined, they were a more practical people, had fewer petty jealousies, and hence a higher estimate of female worth. Still Rome, in this respect, affords a mere fragmentary basis of speculation, for the reason, that the true condition of woman there is not traceable in the life and history of the *many*, but only in the exaggerated memorials of isolated illustrious exceptions.

Turning to the land of the Prophets, the contemplation is happily relieved by the illuminating radiance beaming from the religion of the Bible, to which woman, without controversy, owes her gradual deliverance from the yoke of bondage and oppression. But, even the men of Israel, if left to themselves, would probably have treated their women no better than their idolatrous neighbors, for they were emphatically, what Moses termed them, "stiffed-necked and rebellious." The Almighty himself, however, graciously interposed, to lighten the feminine yoke, and elevate woman to the high pedestal of honor and usefulness, for which she had been originally designed. By Divine appointment, she was called to assist in the construction of the tabernacle—was made acquainted, as well as the sterner sex, with the books of God's law—was made occasionally, too, the recipient of the prophetic spirit, and in some few instances an illustrious instrument of national government. Then, too, was not only her temporal welfare deemed of some account, by allowing her to inherit property, but it was also reduced to a practical demonstration, what in heathen lands scarcely one is willing to admit, namely, that woman, (wonderful to relate,) has *a soul!* And ever since, with the spread of the Gospel of Jesus Christ over the earth, the condition of woman has been on the advance; so that, if woman has done, and is yet doing, much for the Gospel, she is but engaged in liquidating a just debt, for it is not within the compass of figures to portray the blessings the Gospel has conferred on *her!* It cannot admit of debate, however, that it has been reserved for the age, and to a vast extent for the happy country, in which *we* live, to assign to woman a position in the scale of moral, social, and intellectual refinement, such as has never before been awarded to her. Not to *educate* woman now, indeed, is synonomous with a hateful brutality to her. Female reputation is now environed with sanctions, which it is most perilous to invade. The right of woman, in her own proper name, and for her own personal behalf, to acquire and possess property, is a feature stamped upon the statute-books of nearly all the States. Women are no longer kept immersed in solitude, to be brought to the light of heaven, as articles of show, only on extraordinary occasions, but they are both the life and ornament of society. It is now confessed, without provoking a smile, that women have *minds*, as well as men, and that these high capabilities were not conferred on them, to be suffered to lie undeveloped—but should be brought out, like the rough marble from the quarry, and chiseled into forms of symmetry and beauty.

In our own extensive and prosperous commonwealth, (Pennsylvania,) the system of Free Schools has brought the facilities of education in the primary branches to the hearthstones of the poorest and humblest. These Schools of the People—Omnibus Colleges, as we have sometimes called them, swarm with the laughing and jocund juvenile masses. When we see them, at high noon, emptying out their teeming multitudes of living souls—the future fathers and mothers of the republic—we always wonder whether ZECHERIAH, as he looked with a prophet's eye down the long vista of futurity, did not behold this same delightful spectacle in vision, as he wrote: "And the streets of the city shall be full of BOYS and GIRLS, playing in the streets thereof."—(ZECH. v, 8.) But "*Excelsior*" is the cry. The public mind is not content *now* with the means of a primary, limited education. When the branches taught at the common schools have been mastered, there is a demand for loftier and more difficult attainments, and Seminaries, Academies, and Colleges, are founded. Many of these are exclusively devoted to the education of females, where they are taught, by able and experienced professors and teachers, in all the branches of a liberal and thorough education. The happy consequences of which are, that the women of America are now, as they have never been before, educated for pre-eminent usefulness here, and pre-eminent glory and happiness hereafter. A sorrowful reflection, alike upon the intelligence and liberality of the people of Selinsgrove, and of all this prosperous and heaven-blessed region of country, would it have been, if, in this respect, they had been found lagging in the rear of the rest of the world. We hail the establishment of the SUSQUEHANNA FEMALE COLLEGE and of the MISSIONARY INSTITUTE, in this place, therefore, as a high and enduring testimonial to the virtue, the intelligence, the liberality, and the piety of those, who occupy the beautiful and fertile acres which stretch along this noble and majestic river! We hail these two noble Institutions—noble in their conception, and destined to prove nobler still, in their onward march of a generous and expansive utility—as confirmation strong as holy writ, that there beats in your bosoms a yearning parental solicitude for an abundant and adequate supply of all needed educational facilities, alike for your sons and daughters! In these most praiseworthy undertakings, begun and prosecuted amidst so many difficulties, and yet cheered by so many encouragements, we wish you, from our heart's sincerity, full to overflowing, a cordial GOD SPEED! Having put your hands to the plough, may you be enabled to press perseveringly onward, looking to God for constant help, who will assuredly cause refreshing showers to descend even yet more copiously on this great field of spiritual labor—making your Institutions alike the pride and ornament of the Lutheran church--a blessing to the town, the neighborhood, the State, the country, and the world—and causing them to be as overflowing wells in the valley of Bacca, diffusing widespread joy and gladness!

Croakers there are, of course, whose discordant notes are raised, no matter what the object or the occasion, and whom even so distinguished an effort as the elevation of woman cannot silence. We have frequently heard the cry, and hear it yet, that the world is becoming too nice, too polished, too fashionable!—that the young ladies of the present day, so far from being insufficiently educated, are being educated over-much—and that female educational facilities ought hence rather to be diminished, than increased! It is only a very few years since, that we heard a young man assert, with seeming seriousness, that in the choice of a wife *he* would not require any higher standard of intellectual qualification, than that she be sufficiently informed to keep her from *walking into the fire, and to remain in the house during a thunderstorm!* We never ascertained whether, with such a view of female character, and the position his "better half" should occupy in the family, he ever found a wife. It would not at all astonish us, however, if he had found one with entire facility, for he had evidently set up for himself such a contemptibly low standard, that for *him* almost any kind of a woman was too good! But, so far from joining in the cry, by whomsoever uttered, that the women, even of our day, are *over*-educated, we take the liberty of saying, that, in our opinion, they are still not educated half enough. Verily, we do not believe, that the instructions which our sisters and daughters are receiving at these well-conducted and approved institutions — nurturing their faculties, sanctifying their hearts, and preparing them for the duties of earth and the rewards of heaven—could, by any combination of words we might employ, be over-estimated.

Having thus recognized the education of females, on the most liberal and enlarged basis, as an obligation, from which no false logic or perverted philosophy can absolve parents and guardians—addressing ourselves more particularly to the able and beloved President, and the Teachers and Students of the Susquehanna Female College, by whose kind invitation we are engaged in this responsible duty—we shall now proceed to speak of the HELPS and the HINDRANCES to a thorough education of young women. In unfolding these, as the arrangement commends itself both to our taste and convenience, we prefer to reverse the order of the points stated, and will first consider

I. THE HINDRANCES.

Obstacles there exist in the prosecution of this great work, unquestionably, both of a general and specific character, which often serve as most formidable barriers in the way of the student's progress. Those, to which we propose to direct special attention, exist *in the students themselves.* The first we shall name is:

I. *Mental Dissipation.*—The great world-renowned lexicographer, Noah Webster, defines the word dissipate thus: "*Dissipate,* to scatter, to disperse, to drive asunder, to expend, to squander." Thus, we take it, fog is dissipated, scattered, by the wind. Vapor is dissipated, driven asunder, by the rays of the sun. Hence the term has come to be applied, also, to a wild and reckless youth, whom we call "dissipated," for the reason that he expends his patrimony in wasteful prodigality—squanders his time in indolence—wastes his health and strength by ruinous excesses—and his character by vicious and dishonest courses. The popular idea seems to be, that the term applies exclusively to Young Men, and to the outcasts of the other sex. But, keeping the definition of Webster in view, we affirm, it is possible for a young lady to be *very* "dissipated," even during the season of her school-days, and suffer no damage in her reputation, except that which she should sedulously strive to maintain as a diligent and laborious student.

Alas! undeniably true is it, as the history of thousands but too mournfully attests, that a young lady may "dissipate" her time, and the energies of her mind, upon a course of reading, not prescribed by her teacher, and thereby sadly retard her education. King Solomon has said : "Of the making of books there is *no end.*" We wonder what he would say, if he were living now, when books are printed by steam, at the rate of millions a day, and scattered over the earth almost as thickly as the leaves are wafted by the autumnal winds from these beautiful forests? Oh, what a pestiferous nuisance, on a grand scale, are not these myriads of pamphlet sheets, stitched up beneath yellow covers, printed originally, most of them, in Paris and London, and reprinted by the million here! Oh, how fatally ruinous, often, to a sound morality, and always to a well-informed and well-cultivated intellect. We question whether the plagues of Egypt, all told, did half so much injury to the multitudinous dwellers along the Nile, as has been inflicted by the pestilential concoctions of the Paul de Kocks and Eugene Sues, on this and other lands. Not unfrequently, in traveling, have we seen well-dressed, and often quite handsome young ladies, sitting in rail-cars, in the very presence of their parents, intently absorbed in poring over these trashy pages—and always has there been an "irrepressible conflict" within our breast, whether duty did not demand of us to step boldly up to these dissipated girls, and remonstrate against their cramming their young minds with such abominable stuff, and with their over-indulgent pa's and ma's for allowing it. We have not the means of knowing, whether any of this loathsome literary offal ever finds its way up the Susquehanna, but if it should, we trust it may never pollute Susquehanna Female

College. Some young ladies, indeed, are so wedded to these books with the yellow covers, that the relish for them has become a sort of second nature, from which it is as difficult to recover them, as it is to reclaim a drunkard from his cups. Several years ago, the newspapers contained an account of a young lady, a pupil in a Female Seminary in New England, who was gloating over one of these romances, at night, lying in bed, at an hour so late, when the rest of the inmates were all soundly asleep. Deeply absorbed in her favorite reading, sleep at length overcame her, when, horrible to relate, the burning candle fell over, set fire to the bedding, and but for the timely appearance of the night-watch, who saw the flames, and sounded a hasty alarm, the novel-reading Miss would unquestionably have been burned to a crisp!

Our advice to the young ladies of Susquehanna College is, that they read no books whatever, during their scholastic years, not prescribed by their able and learned preceptors—*not even after they have retired to bed, by candle-light!* That they confine themselves, strictly and conscientiously, to their prescribed course of studies, which will prove quite as much, too, as their youthful minds will be able to retain and digest, or as they can crowd into the compass of time allotted to reading and study.

II. The next hindrance in the way of proficiency in your studies, we shall name, is, the "dissipation" incident to the TOILETTE. We would, however, carefully guard our observations on *this* point against misconception. In the discharge of our high office as a Christian Minister, we have never regarded it our duty, (as is the manner of some,) to declaim, with re-iterated vehemence, against any supposed breaches of Christian propriety in the article of personal attire. From this kind of pulpit indulgence we have refrained, for the two-fold reason, that we greatly question its propriety, especially when obtruded upon the audience too frequently; and because we could never promise to ourselves any compensatory return from our labors, since we have lived long enough in the world, to know, that in the affairs of the toilette ladies, after all, do pretty much after their own pleasure, without much regard to the opinions even of their Minister!

Irrespective of these considerations, however, we view our holy Christianity as the generous friend and patron of all that is lovely and attractive even in the outward and material world—the promoter of a chaste and refined taste in every walk and department of life. The Wise King has said: "God has made every thing beautiful in his time."—(Eccl. III, 11.) In the day-time the central luminary of the heavens courses his career on a pathway of unutterable magnificence, through illimitable regions of blue and beautiful ether. At night, the sky is studded with myriads of burning lamps, emblazoned with a jewelry, compared with which the diamond crowns of emperors and queens are darkness itself. The earth, in the spring-time, He adorns with myriads of variegated flowers, most charming to the eye, every one of which eclipses Solomon himself "in all his glory." The forests He attires in a garb of transcendent loveliness, which even in their autumnal semi-nudeness reflect every conceivable light and shade and color. The mountains, even in their ruggedness, extort utterances of astonishment from the beholder; and the ocean is so sublime in the grandeur of its ever-heaving, white-crested billows, that poetry and eloquence and art combined have essayed in vain to furnish an adequate portraiture of its unsurpassed splendors and beauties. Into whatever quarter of the material universe, therefore, we choose to direct our view—mountain, sky, ocean, hill, dale, and valley—our entranced vision is charmed by a boundless exuberance of unutterable beauty and splendor. And if *earth*, groaning and travailing in sin, is so beautiful, what must not *Heaven be*—the chosen metropolis of our glorious and exalted King—the home of the sanctified and saved—where Christ reigns amidst all the splendors of the Mediatorial Throne—where there is light behind light, and glory within glory, in that incomparable refulgence which encompasses the ineffable palace of Jehovah—where the whole infinite art of creation has been employed to manifest the boundlessness of the Divine wisdom and power, even in a material architecture, compared with which the combined glories of the *visible* Universe are but faint shadows, and weak and feeble glimmerings!

With sensibilities always in lively unison with all that is lovely and beautiful in the physical world, as well as in the spiritual, we have hence never lived that day or hour on earth, when we could derive pleasure from pronouncing declamatory phillippics against the fairest of God's intelligent creation, for preferring the beautiful to the homely, even in the selection of their personal attire—always provided, of course, that they avoid ostentatious display and prodigal expense.

Having returned from our aerial voyage, to life's practicabilities, we breathe more freely, and take the responsibility of using plain speech. Be it known to you, then, Young Ladies, that we prefer those of your sex, married or single, who have the means, to dress handsomely—not gaudily, extravagantly, superfluously, for that spoils all—but handsomely and tastefully. Nor do we object to a little jewelry even, if you see fit, provided it be the "pure stuff," and not too much of it, as we do not believe that God has given us these rubies and diamonds to lie buried in ocean's unsounded depths, but for ornament and use.

But we almost fancy that we see some of the learned and erudite theologians, seated around us, shaking their heads, and hear them asking: "What make you of St. Peter, who enjoins it as an article of duty upon christian women, that they shall *not* let their adorning be the *outward* adorning of plaiting the hair, and wearing of gold, or of putting on of apparel—but that they shall let it be the hidden man of the heart in that which is not corruptible, even the ornament of a meek and a quiet spirit, which in the sight of God is of great price." (1 Peter iii, 3, 4.)

Well, we yield to no man, living or dead, in profound respect for the opinions of St. Peter. If we have any favorite among the apostles, it is *he*, and could we suppose that our views were at all in conflict with his, as above enunciated, we would renounce them, utterly and forever. But, according to our interpretation of the passage, we do St. Peter no violence. Most evident is it to us, that he does not argue here against females keeping their hair smoothe, nor of "plaiting" it, if they see fit. Nor does he argue against the selection of handsome material for female dresses, in preference to homely. Nor even against the wearing of gold, (that *is* gold,) or any such thing. Far from it. Peter was a married man. The Scriptures tell us he had a wife, and it is quite likely he had grown up daughters. We assume, then, that this honored Apostle knew full well that interference in the personal attire of his house-hold, to any such extent as *this*, would have been resisted as an invasion of woman's peculiar province, and besides, we think, it would have been beneath an Apostle's dignity! What St. Peter *does* enjoin, however, and enjoins with all becoming seriousness, and with unquestioned propriety, is, that no Christian woman shall ever commit the grievous mistake of supposing, that these external arrangements are her *ornaments*—for they are NOT—but that the true decorations of the Christian woman lie deeper than the surface, even in the "hidden man of *the heart*"—adornments of such high value, that not only the sterner sex would be won by *them* to Christianity, but as to secure the loftiest regards of the Almighty himself. This, it is very plain to us, was what St. Peter meant by the injunction quoted, and nothing more, nothing less.

The young ladies of Susquehanna College are hence at liberty, so far as *we* are concerned, severally to have a looking-glass in their room—sometimes, also, called a mirror! And they are at liberty, too, to stand before them, in the expressive language of St. James, "beholding the natural face in a glass." These privileges, too, we doubt not, they would have all freely exercised, had we granted them or not. But this is our concluding, affectionate, well-meant exhortation on this point, that they remain not before their looking-glasses one second longer than is absolutely required by the exigencies of the case! To be there *often*, and remain there

14

long, will be a willful dissipation of time, and afford demonstrative proof, that their minds are fixed, after all, upon jewelry and dress, and not upon their studies—which must inevitably prove a most formidable barrier to their intellectual progress and proficiency.

III. Under the caption of Hindrances, we can only yet refer to *premature and absorbing alliances*, of a nature so delicate and peculiar, as to render their very introduction hazardous. Against the union of hands, when God has joined the hearts, it would be an anomaly for *us* to declaim, for to minister at Hymen's alter is not an unimportant branch of our sacred office. Many are the hands we have joined, and many the hearts we have made glad, (for a season, at least,) by carrying up vows, uttered on earth, to the registry of heaven. Did we discourage what are called in the matrimonial world "engagements," we would hence be both a pecuniary and professional suicide. We approve of virtuous attachments between the young, after they have arrived at a proper age, even those of opposite sexes—springing up, of course, in a way so purely providential, as that, by no possibility, could they have been avoided. Such attachments, when based on virtuous Christian principles, are a safe-guard, to both parties, against the allurements of the world, in some of their most fascinating forms. So far, then, from discountenancing them in young people, after they have arrived at a proper age, we regard it a most happy circumstance, when a pure affection springs up within them, knitting generous and noble minds in bonds of consentaneous sympathy. Aye, most fortunate do we regard it, when the young of noble principles, and beneficent lives, meet in the same circle, become objects of mutual endearing interest, and by a spontaneous "elective affinity" are irrepressibly drawn to each other.

But, were it in our power, with the deepest seriousness we could command, we would whisper into the ear of every school-girl, the manifest detriment, which all such alliances, prematurely contracted, exercise upon their studies. Too much care cannot be taken, therefore, that they all be put far away from the mind, *until the school-days are ended.* As we ministers are in the habit of saying, "by permission of Divine Providence," they should all be kept at bay, and if Providence will not keep them off entirely, *so long,* then they ought not be suffered to proceed too far! It is a proverb, as trite as it is ancient, that "when poverty comes in at the door, love flies out at the window." We know not how this is, but feel quite certain, that when love enters the College Door, the books are sure to lie neglected! We would have the Young Ladies of Susquehanna Female College bear in mind, therefore, that it is Lindley Murray's *Grammar* they are to be in love with, and not Lindley Murray himself—that it is Pike's *Arithmetic,* upon which their thoughts are to be centered, and not upon Pike—for if they forget, or overlook, these distinctions, it is to be apprehended, they will never receive a diploma, from this Institution, or from any other. We would have them bear in mind, that there is "*a time* for every thing under the sun," and that every duty and concern of life should be performed in its own appropriate season.

Time admonishes us, however, to proceed to the discussion of the second topic of our remarks, which has reference to the auxiliaries that most materially assist young ladies in the prosecution of their studies.

II. THE HELPS.

The first we shall name is *Piety*—a heart washed clean of its sins in the blood of Christ, and delivered of its corruptions by the indwelling, sanctifying power of the Holy Ghost. A most stupendous strengthener of the human intellect, in both male and female, be assured, is Religion. We do not affirm, of course, that Christianity *confers* mind, or even modifies its essential stamina. It no more transforms an ignoramus into a genius, than it changes a dwarf into a giant. But it *does* strengthen, and most powerfully strengthen, the mind, where mind pre-exists, and this it accomplishes in divers ways. One method is, that it offers to its meditations the loftiest and sublimest topics that can possibly be addressed to it—topics, demanding the severest mental discipline and energy. Said the Psalmist: "The entrance of thy words, O Lord, giveth light—it giveth understanding to the simple." (Ps. 119–130.) And said a greater than the Psalmist, even Christ himself: "If thine eye (that is, thine aim,) be single, thy whole body shall be full of light." (MATH. VI, 22.)

We are, of course, well aware, that the chief office of Christianity is to save the soul—to rescue *it* from the darkness and bondage of Satan and of sin, and translate it into the marvelous light and the glorious liberty of the children of God. But this is equally true, that, by indirection, it exercises likewise a most salutary and benign influence on the intellect, and that one of the most valuable of the many accompaniments of a renewed *heart*, is a clearer and more comprehensive *head*. This is an indisputable axiom in mental philosophy, that there is no more efficient strengthener of the intellect, than a renewed heart and a pacified conscience. Whilst we are very far from affirming, Young Ladies, that by your consecrating your hearts to Christ, you will thereby acquire a knowledge of Geography, Botany, Chemistry, History, or Astronomy—but will still have to read and study the books, which treat of these topics—this we *do* affirm, without the fear of successful controversion, that such consecration, whilst it will fit your souls for future felicity and glory, will, likewise, so invigorate and enlarge your *minds*, that you will, with an incalculably augmented relish, comprehend whatever valuable truths are inculcated in any or all of the diversified branches of a complete collegiate education.

Underlying this one great auxiliary, and intimately interwoven with it, are others, which time will only allow us to combine in one associated groupe. They are:

A proper proportion of healthful bodily exercise in the open air, since terrible enemies to successful study are dyspepsia and its concomitants of *ennui* and melancholy:

Avoidance of all irregularities in the habits, alike of eating and fasting, sleeping and waking, so that you do not, like the young lady who read the book with the yellow cover, in bed, by candle-light, convert night into day, and day into night:

Cheerful companions, although never those that are light and trifling, whether in the College Rooms, or elsewhere :

A reverent and becoming respect for your able and worthy preceptors, esteeming them, very highly, in love, for their work's sake :

Punctuality in the performance of every allotted college duty, which involves, also, necessarily, order and method in the proper apportionment of time :

Cleanliness, which is twin-sister to holiness :

Sanctification of the Lord's Day : and, last, but not least,

Honor to parents, which is the first commandment with promise.

All these we regard as so many auxiliaries, whose scrupulous observance cannot fail greatly to facilitate your progress as students, bring to yourselves a rich return of happiness and honor, and confer deserved fame and prosperity upon your *Alma Mater*.

We have now sought to advocate the generous and liberal education of females—sought to demonstrate its incalculable importance and value, both to themselves and to the world—and directed attention to the most prominent HELPS, which serve to promote, and the most formidable HINDRANCES, which serve to retard, this great work. Very imperfectly, however, would our duty, on this occasion, be discharged, if we did not yet, with whatever brevity, seek to elucidate what we understand by the term—female education. Here, Young Ladies, your intellects are to be developed and cultivated. Here knowledge, in all her diversified ramifications, is to unlock her golden store-house to you. Here, too, we trust, your hearts, by the Divine Spirit, are to be improved and sanctified. But duty requires us to state, that there are yet certain other acquirements, indispensable to your future welfare and usefulness, which it is not in the power of your honored preceptors here, however assiduous and able, to impart. Your

2

mission on earth is to be one of UTILITY. You are not to live in the world, mere gilded butterflies, varnished over with a superficial college-gloss—prepared for no higher calling than to figure awhile in Albums and Magazines—pale-faced personifications of tears, love, fainting-spells, poetry, and such like accompaniments of feminine helplessness—to which, if a *practical* man should unhapily become linked, in *real* life, he would inevitably be driven to madness, before the first quarter of the so-called honey-moon. You are not to be prepared here—and we sincerely hope none of you have come here with any such fantastic ideas—to serve as mere decoy-ducks for male sympathy and admiration—receiving, on account of your poetry and fiction, from moustached parasites, mouth-homage, knee-reverence, and *billet-doux* enthusiam, with all their idolatrous concomitants of adulation and incense and nonsense!

Be assured, for all such useless etherealities this age is altogether too stern and too practical. They may answer well enough, by a wise economy of adaptation, to the land Sentiment, bounded by the river Heartlessness, and ruled by the despot Fashion—in which every young man is a coxcomb, and every coxcomb a beau and a flatterer—and every young woman a coquette, and every coquette, in her own estimation, an angel, lacking the wings! In that imperial kingdom, we do not wonder, that every young woman has been carried captive by the hallucination that her eyes are more sparkling than the morning-star—her form fairer than the summer—her teeth whiter than alabaster—her lips ruddier than vermillion—her complexion combining the whiteness of the lily with the incarnation of the rose—and her mind, like a piece of elegant mahogany, just ready to be carved into all sorts of fantastic figures, to be inlaid with ivory and pearl, and silver and gold, and all manner of precious stones! Awaking from this hey-day of fiction and fancy, revery and dreams, only when it is next to impossible to descend from the Mount of Delusion into the Valley of Truth and Fact!

We reiterate, Young Ladies, *you* are to be educated, as

well as we of the sterner sex, for the great mission of *practical life.* Your future arena is to be *in the family,* that earliest and best institution, which is of God's own appointment. For *its* duties you are to be qualified. You are not alone to read and understand your books, but when the binding gives way, and the leaves threaten to come apart, you are to know how to stich them together again—for even, in these days of sewing-machines, a woman, unacquainted with the use of the needle, is as much an anomaly, as would be a professed soldier, ignorant of the use of the sword! Of both parlor and kitchen you are to be the future High Priestesses, ministering with intelligent efficiency at these hallowed domestic altars.

And not there alone, but you are to shine, now and hereafter, in the CHURCH, moving and acting in all the varied fields of Christian benevolence, by lives consecrated to love and duty. You are to weep with them that weep, and rejoice with them that rejoice. In imitation of Him, who suffered and died for mankind, you are to go about, doing good. The fallen you are to lift up. The disconsolate you are to cheer. The hungry you are to feed. The naked you are to clothe. The ignorant you are to instruct. The erring you are to reclaim. The sick you are to solace, and the pillows of the dying you are to smoothe. The cause of Christ, and of suffering humanity, you are to plead—not by declamatory harangues, as some would have you believe, uttered on the corners of the streets—nor by prating about *" Women's Rights "* in town-halls and market-places—but by treading, in silent and unobtrusive meekness, the often stern and rugged path of Duty.

A vastly different life is this from that led in the land of Musing and Dreaming, and you must not expect to be equipped for its requirements simply by what you shall study and acquire *here,* however valuable these acquisitions. No! These lessons are to be gained in the great world-wide school of Experience, amidst the cares and solicitudes of your after-years—often in the disciplining school of life's bitterest trials and adversities. The capacity to meet these requirements is to be gained, too, from the patient study of God's Word, and in fervent and frequent invocations of God's grace, which descends, with chastening and subduing gentleness, from the shining temples of the upper sanctuary. Seek ye, then, *moral* and *spiritual* improvement and elevation, even with a ten-fold more absorbing intensity than you do literary and intellectual. Great are your responsibilities. Numerous and diversified will be your opportunities for doing good. Oh! array not, then, the artillery of your influence, now or hereafter, on the side of Sin and Folly, but on the side of Virtue, Truth, Mercy, and Religion! Acting thus—improving and elevating yourselves, and laboring for the elevation and improvement of others—hundreds, if not thousands, will be benefitted, both for time and for eternity, by the beauty of your character, and the force and lustre of your example. Men, women, and children, conscious of how much, under God, they owe to You, instead of showering upon you unmeaning adulation for external and adventitious charms, will render you the homage of a sincere and abiding Gratitude, for the lovely and heaven-born spirit that dwells *within*. And, though your names may never be gazetted, like those of conquering captains and heroes, over the earth—and may never be sounded with pæans of applause in triumphal processions—you will be, in the highest and holiest sense, ministering angels *at home*. And, having thus, each in her allotted sphere, faithfully and conscientiously done and suffered the holy and righteous will of God on earth, in heaven you will " *shine as the brightness of the firmament and as the stars forever and ever.*"

A N

ADDRESS,

Delivered November 9, 1859,

ON THE OCCASION OF THE DEDICATION OF THE

MISSIONARY INSTITUTE,

IN SELINSGROVE, PA.

BY

REV. DANIEL STECK, A. M.

PASTOR OF ST. JOHN'S EV. LUTHERAN CHURCH,

LANCASTER, PA.

———⋅✦⋅———

BALTIMORE:
PUBLISHED BY T. NEWTON KURTZ,
151 WEST PRATT STREET.
1859.

REV. DANIEL STECK'S ADDRESS.

Christian Brethren and Friends :

It is no ordinary occasion which has brought us together to-day. We have assembled in this holy temple, for the purpose of dedicating publicly and solemnly, to the great end for which it has been founded, *The Missionary Institute of the Ev. Lutheran Church.* One year ago, drawn by the interest we felt in an enterprise on which, however it might be regarded by men, God was manifestly smiling, many of us were here to witness the induction of our venerable friend, the Superintendent, and that of our esteemed brother, his worthy associate, into the high official positions with which the Board of Directors had honored them. It was "a high day" in Zion ; and the children of Zion were "glad with exceeding joy." God had blessed his servants ; he had prospered the work of their hands ; he had given them a token for good. Hence "the people praised him ; yea, all the people praised him." Thus, I say, it was, when for the purpose just mentioned, many of us convened in this sanctuary, one year ago.

But now we have met together to rejoice in additional tokens of the divine goodness. What was then auspiciously begun, has by the blessing of God, so far succeeded as to place its ultimate success, beyond all peradventure. During the year a most encouraging number of candidates for the gospel ministry have been under training for the holy office ; and yonder graceful edifice, to whose halls they and their successors, eager to obtain the knowledge which is to fit them for their work, will hereafter resort, is now to be set apart to the great purpose for which it has been reared. Surely if ever the friends of this enterprise have had occasion for thankfulness they have to-day. It is meet that every one of them should say with *peculiar* emphasis, "Bless the Lord O my soul, and all that is within me bless his holy name; bless the Lord O my soul, and forget not all his benefits."

But not to indulge in these felicitations, however suitable they may be to the time, I will proceed without further delay, to the execution of the task which my friends of the Board, in their too great partiality, have imposed upon me. I wish here to say that in making choice of a subject, it was my desire to select one, which, in its nature, would not be foreign to the great interests which centre in the Institute. And I would add that if in the remarks I have to offer, I should reiterate in substance much that has been well and eloquently said by the distinguished men who have spoken on the general subject on former occasions, I have no apology to offer other than this, that many things were said on those occasions which no man need be ashamed to appropriate, and which will bear to be repeated while the world shall stand.

I propose, then, to consider the Missionary Institute with respect to *Its Origin, Its Genius, Its Prospects,* and *Its Claims.*

I. The Origin of the Missionary Institute.—The Institute has become a fact. It is among the things that *are.* It has "a local habitation and a name." And the question touching the *cause* of its existence is easily answered. It is the result of a great want—a want which has been long and extensively acknowledged, and not only acknowledged, but mourned over by thousands and tens of thousands of God's people in this land—I mean the want of ministers to preach the everlasting gospel of Jesus Christ to perishing sinners. On all sides and among all denominations we have heard the cry, and we hear it as emphatically to-day as at any former time, "The harvest is great, but the laborers are few: Lord send forth laborers into the harvest." But if this want has been great among our brethren of the Presbyterian, Episcopal, Baptist, Methodist, and other churches, it has been preeminently so among us.

The truth of this assertion is so manifest to every one at all acquainted with our denominational history in this country, that it needs no formal proof. The want of faithful ministers among us is very great. It has always been so. There never has been a period from the first planting of the Lutheran church on this continent, down to the present time, when the number of its ministers has been any thing like adequate to the demand for ministerial service. From the day that the patriarch Muhlenberg first landed on these western shores even to this passing hour, the church of our choice has been retarded in its growth and impaired in almost all respects, as the result, among other causes, of this great . evil.

But it may be said that the absence of colleges and theological seminaries for so long a period in our history will account for the fact that the number of ministers has fallen so far below the wants of the people. That much of the evil is traceable to this fact, we frankly and cheerfully admit; but that this fact is sufficient of *itself* to account for the deficiency we do as resolutely deny. The ground of our denial is simply this: we have colleges and theological seminaries at the present time, and we have had some of them for the last quarter of a century and more; and yet it is doubtful whether the disproportion between the number of our ministers and the extent of our population, is not greater now than it has been at any former period of our denominational existence in this land. What then? Have our existing institutions, so far as this question is concerned proved a failure? Have they done nothing to supply the church with ministers? God forbid that we should say so. They have not proved a failure. They have done much to supply the church with ministers, able ministers of whom she has a right to be proud. But this they have not done; (nor is the failure chargeable to any fault of theirs;) they have not sent them forth in sufficient numbers. We go further. We hazard the assertion, that notwithstanding all their excellencies, all their unquestioned and unquestionable claims to the gratitude, the confidence, and the patronage of the people, they are not likely, even though they were placed under the most favorable auspices, to be able to supply the requisite ministerial force for a great while to come.

In order to present a more vivid picture of the destitution of which I have been speaking, permit me to take a momentary glance at those portions of the country in which the Lutheran church is principally found. Pennsylvania, which is known to be the strong-hold of Lutheranism in America, contains about 300 Lutheran ministers, about 740 churches, and about 82,000 communicants. Of these 300 ministers we will say 250 are pastors. This would give an average of nearly three congregations to one pastor, a number entirely too large, as all must see, to allow the possibility of his being able to do justice to them. Assuming that the proper average would be two congregations to one pastor, then, in our own State, where we are accustomed to think but little destitution exists, we need nearly *one-third* more ministers than are now found within her territory. But this calculation embraces only the regularly organized churches; it does not include the large number of stations where the word is occasionally preached, and other openings for missionary labor in countless localities all over this great commonwealth. In this direction then we find an ample, and at the same time most interesting field for at least one hundred laborers more. So that the necessities of our church in Pennsylvania alone, demand this day an increase of not less than 200 additional ministers. In other words, if the supposition be correct, that we have 1,000 acting pastors in the whole Lutheran church of North America, the one-half of this entire force might be concentrated within the limits of this single State and that without any danger of crowding the field.

The other States in which the Lutheran church has considerable strength are, New York, Maryland, the two Carolinas, Virginia, Ohio, Indiana and Illinois. Of course this view has respect to the church as embraced in the General Synod. What then must be said of the want of ministers within the limits of the States just named? I am not able to speak on this point with the precision of accurate calculation; but I presume, in order to meet the demands of the church on the general territory indicated, its ministerial force ought to be augmented, at least, in an equal degree. That is, it ought to be increased by about one-third.

But in addition to all this, look at the immense Home Missionary work which remains to be done in the States of New Jersey, Iowa, Wisconsin, Michigan, Kentucky, Tennessee, Georgia, Alabama, Mississippi, Texas, and California; to say nothing of the Territories of Kansas and Nebraska; nor of the Canadas; nor of lonely yet pleading Nova Scotia. Thus from the north, from the south, from the east, from the west, we hear the cry, "Send us ministers! send us ministers!!" It has become a mighty cry, and it is mightier to-day than it ever was before; and it imposes a mighty responsibility; and if it wake not a slumbering church to appropriate action, will not the blood of souls who have perished by her neglect be found upon her hands when the great day of reckoning comes? And yet shall we be told that a destitution so great, so wide-spread, and so ruinous in its results, does not justify the inauguration of a special instrumentality for its removal? And, as if this were not enough, shall men who can prove their title to the gratitude of the church by a long career of earnest devotion to her welfare, who have literally grown gray in her service, and who cannot consent to die without leaving behind them some special proof of their concern for her continued well-being, be hindered in the prosecution of a great and wise design, and not only so, but *paraded* before the world as though they were the veriest enemies of the cause they profess to have so earnestly at heart? Surely this ought not so to be!

Hitherto I have spoken of the want of ministers at home. But let us not forget the claims of 600,000,000 of the race who live beyond the great waters, and on the islands of the seas. These are still as destitute of gospel light as though not a single ray from that divine sun had ever fallen upon the darkness of our world. While other denominations are laboring with commendable diligence to save those benighted millions, shall we shrink from the duty, or lightly esteem the glory of bearing our full share in the great redeeming work? I bless God that we have missionaries in the foreign field; and who does not wish we had more of them there? Perhaps the subject is too sacred to allow any thing like an appeal to denominational pride, and I shall make no such appeal; but is it not proper, that the church which makes it her boast that she is the eldest daughter of the Reformation, should aspire to at least an equality in effort with other churches less honored by age than she in extending the blessings of salvation to the perishing millions of earth? Who of us does not long to see the coming of that day when faithful missionaries of our American Lutheran Zion shall unfold the glad tidings of the gospel to the swarming millions of China; and when they shall plant the standard of the cross at every commanding point along the Asiatic coast, and in every idolatrous nation among whom Providence may open a door of entrance? Who of us, when he pleads with God for the conversion of the heathen, would not say, "Lord remember and bless *our* missionaries there?" And when the last trump shall announce the end of all things, and the several branches of the great army shall respectively exhibit the result of their operations in the mighty mystic battle, who of us would not exult to see the church in which our fathers worshiped, and labored, and died, sharing a glorious part in the honors of that notable day?

Thus, this consideration unites with those which have gone before, in the demand for ministers. We must have them by hundreds on hundreds, otherwise we shall never be able to accomplish the work to which the "Great Head of the Church" is calling us. The great want is a great increase of ministers, to preach God's great gospel. And in *this* want the Missionary Institute has had its origin.

II. THE GENIUS OF THE MISSIONARY INSTITUTE claims in the next place a brief notice. By the genius of the Institute I mean its *peculiar character* as a school for the training of candidates for the gospel ministry. As a theological institution it, of course, possesses some features in common with all other seminaries of this class. Still, it comes before the world, as a school of our American church, with characteristics which make it, in a good measure, a peculiar institution of the general class to which it belongs. It is peculiar,

First, in regard to the *age* and other *relations* of the men it proposes to educate. These, according to the language employed in the "Statutes," are "pious and sound-minded men irrespective of age or domestic ties." True, our existing seminaries have, in some instances, admitted men considerably advanced in years, and burdened with family cares; and they have admitted them with no higher preparatory advantages than those of a good common school education; and having done what they could for them, during a brief sojourn of two years, they sent them forth respectable and useful ministers of the New Testament. But when men of this character are received, it is done by a virtual suspension of the rule by which the admission of candidates is regulated. Such men are, by the existing regulations, made and *meant* to be, an exceptional class, if, indeed, their admission can be legally claimed at all. Though they are, in many instances, pre-eminently fitted to become useful ministers, they cannot but feel that, as students in schools designed for another class, they are *tolerated* rather than desired. This I say in no spirit of censure, but rather in the spirit of praise. Let our higher institutions be true to the great end for which they have been founded. Let them aim at giving to the young men, entrusted to their care, the most finished and thorough education of which they are capable. This is what the church expects of them; and she is grateful, as she ought to be, for the measure in which her expectations in this regard have been realized.

But here is an Institution which interposes no barrier, either expressed or implied, to the admission of students of the class under consideration. It welcomes them. It specifies them in its "Statutes" and tells them it wants them to

come. It was *made* for them. It is emphatically *their* Institution. Hence, as students in it, they will feel perfectly at
home. All its associations will be congenial and happy.

But is it likely that any considerable number of men, such
as we are now describing, will resort to this Institute for the
purpose of enjoying the advantages it is prepared to afford?
We answer yes, it is likely; and if the proper efforts are
made by pastors and others, it is certain to be the case. Who
does not know that many men, of fine natural endowments
and respectable education, are converted after they are 25 or
30 years of age! Who, among our faithful and laborious
pastors, has not met with many instances of such conversion,
especially during those blessed seasons of revival with which
our church, of late years, has been so extensively favored?
And who has not noticed that these converts are often filled
with an irrepressible desire to glorify God in the work of
the ministry? And now that an institution for the special
accommodation of such men, has been established, what is
there to hinder them from resorting to it in numbers so large
as, in the result, to cause many a moral "desert" within
the limits of our long-neglected Zion, to "blossom like the
rose?" Let pastors and people be observant of the indications of providence in this particular, and the Institute will
soon be thronged with students of the class now had in view.
There is a speciality,

Secondly, in the *adaptation* of the course of instruction to
be pursued in the Institute, to what may be considered the
actual *necessities* of the men who are to be trained for the
holy office in it. The duration of their connection with it is
made dependent on the extent of their attainments at the
time of their reception. The entire course embraces three
years, but it may be cut down to two, or one, or less, in accordance with the contingency just named. As a matter of
fundamental regard, it will be the constant aim of the Institute to furnish the church with men who shall prove themselves to be well-grounded in the great essential doctrines of
the Christian system—men who shall be deeply versed in the

Bible; and, regarding the Bible as the *ne plus ultra* of their Theology, shall be able, in the spirit and power and propriety of true embassadors of the Holy One, to proclaim its great redeeming doctrines to the world. If the Institute shall prove true to this aim, the students will not commit the common folly of giving themselves to pursuits, where, as the French proverb says "the grains will not pay for the candle," and where the philosopher and the scholar threaten to swallow up the pastor and the divine.

But we sometimes hear it said that men, trained in accordance with the genius of this new Institution, will hardly be able to render efficient service in the ministry. Of course we have no manner of sympathy with this objection. We scarcely consider it as entitled to the respect of a serious reply. But look at it for a moment. The essential elements of real efficiency in the work of the ministry—what are they? They are such as these: *First, True Piety*, involving the practical renunciation of all known sin and the consecration of soul and body, life and being, for time and eternity to the service and glory of God. This is an element of efficiency, and it is fundamental. There can be no real efficiency without it. A *Second* element is *good sense*. This, too, is fundamental. A man lacking in this quality, however great his attainments may be in other respects, is not likely to be successful in any profession, and, least of all, in the ministry. A *Third* element is *familiar acquaintance with God's great scheme for saving sinners*—that is, the gospel of Jesus Christ. This a man must understand and know how to unfold and apply in order to be successful. A *Fourth* element is *facility and force in the communication of truth*, "aptness to teach," as it is styled by the Apostle; or, as the people say, a man to be efficient in the pulpit must be "*a good speaker.*" These elements respect the *man*, and where they meet in the same person, assuming of course that the necessary divine influence is not withheld, there will be success, and no power on earth or in hell can prevent it. And the friends of the Missionary Institute, I take it for granted, will have an eye to the question—whether these elements meet, or are *likely* to meet in the men they may wish to send here to be educated.

But, all theorizing and argumentation aside, it is a fact established by history, and plain every-day observation, that men, not trained in the highest style of the schools—nay, men who are not "College bred" in any sense, are in many instances among the ablest, most successful, and most influential ministers in the church. And if this is a fact, what ground is there to question the adaptation of an educational enterprise like this to the development of the most glorious results, both for the church and the world ?

About the year 1795* the celebrated Dr. Bouge established the Missionary Seminary at Gosport, England. In that Institution he was the sole instructor. No edifice was erected, but the students resided in different families, and met daily for recitation at the vestry adjoining the church. At that Institution Dr. Bouge, in his life, without any assistant teacher, educated more than four hundred ministers. Among these was the Rev. John Angel James, a man of God whose name will be fragrant among Christians to the end of time, whose "Anxious Inquirer" led some of us to Jesus when our sins lay like a mountain on our hearts; and who now, having finished his course, has exchanged a life of incessant and successful toil in the Master's vineyard here, for a crown of ever-during glory at God's right hand in heaven. Another was the celebrated Dr. George Bennet, of London. Another was the illustrious Dr. Morrison, who translated the whole Bible into the Chinese language,—not to mention other names fit to be placed in the brightest galaxy of the great and good, by whose instrumentality God has blessed the church and the world. It will not do, therefore, to question the adaptation of this new enterprise to the attainment of the end for which it has been founded. The plan has been tried and it has proved successful.

Besides, is there any thing in the nature of the case to pre-

---

* *The very year* at the beginning of which the Founder and Superintendent of the Ev. Luth. Missionary Institute *was born.*

vent a large proportion of the men who shall pursue their studies here, from being, in the proper sense of the expression, men of learning? Their attainments may not be as extensive, at the close of their term of study, as are those of many who are educated at other institutions; but what is an education, obtained at our very best institutions, other than a mere rudimental process? Is it not just meant to give the student a good start? This, as every intelligent person must allow, is the theory. Admit it, and it will follow that, although the men who are trained here may not, at the time of leaving the Institution, be quite even with some others, yet, if throughout the whole of their after life they address themselves to studies appropriate to their calling, and observe, in their prosecution, the two essentials of a just method and a becoming zeal, they must, in the progress of years, become men of extensive learning—men to whom, under God, the church can afford to entrust her highest and most sacred interests. Though hindmost in the start, they may be first at the goal; and this often turns out to be the case in fact. Who has not known young men who have enjoyed the best educational advantages, while reposing on their past attainments, and relaxing their efforts, totally eclipsed by the brilliant career of others who, destitute of the advantages enjoyed by the former, were forced by circumstances, or led by choice, to throw themselves on their own resources? We have all known instances of the kind. They are to be met with everywhere. Assuming, then, that the preparatory training, afforded by the Missionary Institute, may be less extensive, in some respects, than that which may be obtained in institutions of higher pretention, we nevertheless hold that there is good ground for the persuasion that, of the men who are to go forth from this same Institute, the church will hereafter be glad to recognize many of her ablest and most accomplished ministers.

But I would not be understood as implying that the men we need are men of mere book-learning. There is among us "too much faith in the intellectual letter, and too little in

3

the moral life. There is mighty faith in worn-out and thread-bare technicalities, and new-made creeds. We believe that the people of the land are waiting for a Christianity warm from the cross of Jesus—such a Christianity will not be in vain in its preachings. What is needed is not mere intellectual sympathy and training, but moral sympathy— moral discipline; these are the only mighty teachers—these are the unfailing professors. The ministers we need are those who have the impress of the finger of God and the cross of Jesus burnt into their souls—ministers baptized with the Holy Ghost and with fire,—clear, bright-eyed men, able to look through the heart of error; strong-hearted men, upon whom the sorrowing may lean for support; men of the gifted eye and gifted tongue; men of the self-denying frame, who shall be able to convince the world—the trading, hux- tering world, that conscience is not a chattel or a commodity, but a magnet and a life. These men *must* come. Whence *will* they come? Come they from College, Institute, or Cob- bler's stall, forward will we press and say,—*Brothers, all hail!!"*

III. THE PROSPECTS OF THE MISSIONARY INSTITUTE.—This is the next topic, and we will devote a brief space to its consid- eration. Whatever we may say concerning the prospects of this enterprise, at the present stage of its developments, it will be admitted that it *has* had difficulties to encounter, and that these have been neither few in number nor inconsidera- ble in magnitude. Some of our most prominent and influen- tial ministers have, from the beginning, stood forth in the most open and determined hostility against it. The reasons for their hostility we need not mention. They are known to all; for they have been proclaimed throughout the length and breadth of the church. Nor is it for me to say that this opposition is not the result, in many cases, of an honest dif- ference of opinion. That such is the fact I have not the shadow of a doubt. I wish, from the bottom of my heart, that I could find ground for the persuasion that the whole of the opposition of which I am speaking could be accounted for on a supposition so rational, so manly, and at the same time so Christian. There was a time, and it is still fresh in the recollection of us all, when, as the result of the almost universal outcry against the enterprise, he alone, who is its Founder, as it would seem, had the courage to stand up for it and speak in its defence. But, in this respect, its early history has not been peculiar. The same thing has been true, in some degree, of almost every meritorious undertaking since the world began. I may not multiply examples, but I will mention one. When Jerusalem lay in ruins, and the returned captives were seen lingering in mournful groups amid the confused and sightless heaps which every where met the eyes and saddened the hearts of the hapless beholders, the God of heaven sent Nehemiah from the royal palace of Shushan to the land of his fathers for the purpose of reconstructing the demolished walls of Jerusalem, and of causing the city of David, now a heap of mouldering ruins, to become once more a praise in the earth. Noble, heroic man! I see him now. He has just returned from his lonely nocturnal survey of the mighty desolation. His great soul is moved, and he can no longer bear to hold his peace. He stands in the presence of his countrymen, and the deep feelings of his heart, finding egress in the words of his lips, he says: *"Ye see the distress that we are in—how Jerusalem lieth waste, and the gates thereof are burned with fire ; come, and let us build the wall of Jerusalem, that we be no more a reproach."* And among the people there are those who reply in the same noble spirit, saying, *" Let us rise up and build."* And, suiting their actions to their words, at it they go. But instantly enemies rise up in determined and desperate opposition against them. Ridicule, denunciation, violence, every conceivable form of opposition, is employed to defeat the great undertaking. Nevertheless good Nehemiah goes right on with his work, and, with a faith which would have done honor to Abraham himself, he comforts his soul and the souls of his friends by saying, *" The God of heaven, he will prosper us; therefore we, his servants, will arise and build."* He did prosper them, and their faith in the God of their fathers was vindicated in the triumphant success with which he crowned the work of their hands.

So it has been with the Missionary Institute. It has likewise met with the most determined opposition. But the cause has had its Nehemiah in the person of the venerable Superintendent, who, convinced of the importance of the undertaking, sought to encourage the few friends who came to his help by saying, "*The God of heaven, he will prosper us ; therefore we, his servants, will arise and build.*" Onward accordingly they went in the prosecution of their great work ; and, notwithstanding the jeers and hard sayings of the Sanballasts and Tobias, of whom the whole land seemed to be full, the success of the good cause could not be defeated. God, as it soon appeared to many, was viewing it with favor, and seeing upon it, as they thought, the seal of *his* approbation, they could not do otherwise than place themselves among the number of its friends. Thus it is apparent that the darkest days, and most trying vicissitudes of the Missionary Institute have passed away ; while the faith, courage, and perseverance of its early friends are about to be crowned with the most gratifying success. Prejudice, hostility, and the various forms of antagonism are losing much of their intensity, and making room for the dominancy of a better and more liberal spirit.

It is worthy of remark that this enterprise, from its very inception, has met with great favor among our more pious, intelligent and enterprising laymen. Perceiving as they do the immense destitution which prevails, and seeing no reasonable hope of its speedy supply by the agencies which have heretofore been in opposition, they almost every where hail the Institute, not only as a useful appendage to existing instrumentalities, but, under the circumstances of the times, as a manifest and imperious necessity. Hence they are found speaking in its favor, praying for its success, and contributing, unasked, of their means to keep it in operation. This, assuredly, is a most significant fact, and it argues well for the prospects of the Institute.

Nor should it be forgotten, in this connection, that during the past year, the first year of its existence, an unexpectedly large number of candidates for the ministry have been undergoing a course of instruction, preparatory to their future work. This newly-erected "School of the Prophets," has to-day, beyond all doubt, the largest number of students contained in any Lutheran Theological Seminary, within the bounds of the General Synod. Who would have predicted such a result one year ago? Was it not beyond the hope of the most enthusiastic friend? And did not many say, in substance at least, it could not be? But what none were prepared to look for in this respect, God, in his all-wise providence, has brought to pass, thus reminding us of the inspired saying: "*And thou Bethlehem in the land of Juda, art not the least among the princes of Juda.*" Taking, therefore, this result of the past year's operations as a basis on which to calculate for the future, what may not be expected from this newly-inaugurated enterprise? Surely it must be admitted that never, in the history of our church in this land, has any similar undertaking been commenced which gave so many early indications of speedy and enlarged success.

These being our convictions, we are constrained to claim for this Institute, so long misunderstood by many, the opening of a prospect replete with the most flattering assurances of a glorious future. The many and fervent prayers which are constantly going up to God in its behalf, both from the pulpits of the churches, and the fire-sides of the people; the strong hold it has secured in the confidence of our pious and enterprising laity, and the substantial sympathy it is every where eliciting from them; the manifest favor it finds at the hands of a large proportion of our most devoted and successful pastors, and the promptness with which they stand up in the advocacy of its claims; the encouraging number of students already in process of training for the work of the ministry, and the intelligence we have that the number is likely soon to be greatly enhanced: these considerations, together with others of a like encouraging character, but which may not now be specified, betoken the hand of God in the establishment of the Missionary Institute, and promise for it a career of extensive usefulness.

IV. THE CLAIMS OF THE MISSIONARY INSTITUTE.—This is the only remaining point of the general subject to be considered; nor need we spend much time in its discussion. We put the question then, *Is not this institution, both in view of its character and design, entitled to the confidence and sympathy of the whole church?* Our answer is neither equivocal nor cold, but explicit and hearty—we say *yes!* it is entitled to the confidence and sympathy of the church; and if called on to defend our position we would base its vindication, among others, upon such grounds as the following:

First. The church has long ago sent forth its verdict endorsing the *principle* of the Institute. I do not say that this verdict has been unanimous, but I do affirm that it has been so general as to justify us in claiming it as the judgment of the church at large. It is well known that a few years ago, one of our most influential Synods, not only endorsed the *principle*, but went so far in its synodical capacity as to take some primary steps to carry out the *thing* itself. That same Synod was among the first to move in the important matter of forming the General Synod. It was also in advance of the other Synods in efforts to establish our noble institutions at Gettysburg. To it also must be awarded the honor of having been foremost in the formation of our general societies for Education and Missions. It was entirely proper, therefore, that a prominent member of that Synod should, some eight or ten years ago, in his capacity as President, when preaching the Synodical Sermon, compare his Synod with the children of Issachar, of whom it is said that they were *"men that had understanding of the times, to know what Israel ought to do."* It was a happy conception, that, of the ingenious preacher; and the compliment paid to the Synod was deserved. They have been a sagacious tribe in our American Israel. They "knew what Israel ought to do." Nor did those sons of Issachar forfeit their claims to pre-eminence in the matter of *understanding the* wants of *the times*, when a few years ago they declared themselves in favor of the establishment of just such an institution as the one we are now in the act of dedicating. Never did they express themselves more wisely, more Issachar-like, than they did on that occasion. I refer, of course, to the Synod of Maryland. And it is well known that other Synods, in various sections of the church, have been equally explicit in their endorsement of this long-cherished principle, this conviction which has fastened itself so deeply and immovably upon the mind of the church. It is true that in some instances strenuous efforts have been made to obtain synodical action, and action in other forms, adverse to this principle; but in no instance, so far as my knowledge extends, have such efforts been attended with much success. The conviction, therefore, has been wide-spread and overwhelming, that a special agency like that of the Institute is needed, in order to fill up the meager ranks of the ministry in our beloved but suffering Zion.

To-day we are here, not to reiterate a long-felt and oft-expressed conviction that something is needed, but to rejoice in the happy realization of the thing itself. And now that the " principle," the " good idea," about which men have so long talked, stands before us in the form of a living result, should not the whole church rally around it and yield it a most cordial support? Surely, if the " principle" is good, the thing itself is better. This is one of the grounds of our vindication.

Secondly, we hold that this enterprise, now so auspiciously commenced, deserves the confidence and support of all the friends of our venerated Zion, *on the ground of its purpose distinctly avowed to rely at all times on God and his people, for the* MEANS *whereby it hopes to move forward in the execution of its great mission.* The men to whom under God it owes its existence, commenced their work in prayer and faith; and they have carried it on in the same spirit to this day. They love their work. Every pulsation of their hearts beats in unison with it. It is a work for the church. It is a work for God. Nor does the enterprise ask to be put in any position before the world, other than that which involves the necessity of constant dependence on divine aid. It does not ask to live a day longer than it can live usefully; not an hour longer than God and his church shall deign to favor it. When it can no longer prove its right to live by the results of its life, it will be content to die and be remembered no more. It hopes to live and to live long; but be its life long or short, it is determined to "*live by faith.*" "THE LORD WILL PROVIDE:" surely this is a noble motto, and it is the motto which from the beginning has been emblazoned upon the banner of the Missionary Institute. Nor have the results of the past failed to vindicate the policy involved in the great life principle thus announced. The cause has been sustained; and the means in many instances have come to hand in ways so remarkable as to indicate the presence of a power more than human—as to prove beyond a doubt the operation of the finger of God.

And now I ask whether a cause which can rest so implicitly on God and his people for support, which asks not that any extraordinary provision be made to-day for such wants as the distant future may require, which simply looks for the supply of present necessities and is persuaded that it will never look in vain :—I ask whether such a cause does not give evidence of the most thorough consciousness of its own intrinsic rectitude; and I ask whether such a cause does not commend itself to the confidence and substantial sympathy of the friends of our Zion every where? For my own part I cannot resist the conviction that this peculiarity of the enterprise must ever commend it to the approval of both God and men.

Thirdly, we maintain that the *character of the men the Institute proposes to send forth entitles it to the confidence and support of the church.* These are "men of tried piety and good common sense; too far advanced in life and too slenderly furnished with pecuniary means to admit of their passing through what is called a full course of education." The object is to "give them such a literary and theological training as will qualify them to become sound historical, biblical, and practical preachers, and efficient pastors." It is believed that there are hundreds of faithful and intelligent laymen in the church, "ardently desirous to go forth in the name of the Lord to tell the story of the cross to perishing sinners and build up the waste places of our Zion. But not adequately instructed, and finding no suitable provision for them to obtain the requisite qualifications, they are unfortunately shut out from the work to which they feel God has appointed them; and to their own ineffable grief and the incalculable loss of the church, they are doomed to smother the holiest and loftiest aspiration of their heart in ignoble obscurity, and pass on to the grave in comparative inactivity and uselessness." Such in brief is the character of the men here to be trained for the holy and blessed work of the ministry. Thus will there be introduced "upon the unguarded walls of Zion squadron after squadron of brave and hardy watchmen, perhaps in some respects less gorgeously furnished than others, but not less necessary and efficient, nor less faithful and devoted in their peculiar sphere." O, how much we need such men, earnest warm-hearted men, men of mighty faith and burning zeal, to fill up the attenuated ranks of the sacramental host. We need them every where. From city and town, from hill and valley, from every section of this broad commonwealth, "the homestead and heritage of Lutheranism in America;" yea, and from beyond, from every quarter of this immense confederacy, there comes the cry, "Send us ministers, men of God who have been 'baptized with the Holy Ghost and with fire,' and who have 'determined not to know any thing among men, save Jesus Christ and him crucified.'" Such men are in demand every where; and come they *must;* and come they WILL. That Eye omniscient which discerned the prophet among the herdmen of Tekoah, will find them out; and that Voice Divine which summoned Saul of Tarsus from the high-way of Damascus, will call them forth. That eye is on them now, and that voice distinct as the battle cry of the warrior chief, on the eve of some mighty conflict, is ringing the solemn summons in their ears. And the men are coming : from the workshops, from the fields, from the counting-houses, from all the avocations of life they are coming obedient to the voice of the Captain of our salvation, "his sword upon his thigh" and "his vesture dipped in blood." Yes, they are coming, and thank God some of them are here to-day, putting on their armor and preparing themselves for the mighty yet bloodless battle to which the Great Captain is calling them.

And I ask once more whether an enterprise which aims to increase the number of our ministry by the addition of such men to its ranks, men of clear heads, and warm hearts, and earnest souls, is not entitled to the confidence and support of the whole church? Must not every thoughtful man yield to this question his most cordial Yea, and Amen?

And now, in conclusion, let me congratulate the Board of Managers on the happy results which have thus far crowned their efforts, and as well, on the auspicious prospects which are before them. Prompted by an abiding conviction that such an enterprise was a necessity of the times—a conviction which you shared only in common with many thousands of our people all over this land, you resolved in reliance on divine aid, and for the purpose of promoting the glory of God, to establish this new "school of the prophets." The help for which you prayed has not been withheld. The God of heaven has been with you. He has crowned your labors with great success; and if you remain true to your high trust his hand will continue to be with you ; and the institution you dedicate this day will be a monument to your honor, and a blessing to the world.

Allow me further to felicitate you on the goodness of God in preserving the life and health of our venerable friend, whom we all alike honor as the Founder of the Institute, and whom you still retain at its head. We all know with what ardor, ability, and success he has devoted his past life to the best interests of our church—a church whose annals, adorned with illustrious names, but wait the result of the days and deeds which yet remain to him, to receive *his* name high on the immortal scroll. You are peculiarly fortunate in having a man of his ability, energy, and experience to preside over your cherished institution. And that he may yet live many years to aid in the training of your students and lend to the cause the influence of his name, will be our earnest and united prayer.

Nor can I forbear to congratulate you on your good fortune in securing the services of our esteemed brother, his worthy associate. We have all known him well. From the commencement of his ministry his hand has been active in every good work. He has made himself known as a man of progress. He has been especially zealous, and perseveringly active in the great cause of Missions, both Home and Foreign. Connected as he has been, at various times, with several Synods in our State, he has never failed to manifest the most lively interest in the momentous question which demands the extension of the knowledge of Jesus Christ, not only among the destitute in our own land, but among the perishing in heathen lands. To him, perhaps, more than to any other person of his years, are we indebted for the interest which is now felt on this subject, especially among the churches in this State. Being deeply interested in this subject, and knowing the extent of its claims upon us as a people, he is pre-eminently fitted to infuse an ardent and enlightened missionary spirit among the students who from time to time, shall place themselves under his instruction.

Go on, then, brethren, in the earnest fulfillment of your great mission. As in the beginning you had for your motive the glory of God and the welfare of men, so let the same be your polar star in all time to come. You will be duly mindful of the fact that the age in which we live is one of progress. Let PROGRESS, progress in the right direction be your watchword in the management of the Missionary Institute. Let it be understood that your true vocation is to train for the church, to serve her in the ministry, earnest, intelligent, courageous men of God—men who shall both understand their duty and be ready to give their hands and their hearts to its performance. Let them be men imbued with the true spirit of Revivals. What are we as a church to-day in all that makes us a power for good in this land, that we do not owe to the spirit of revivals? May the time never come when it shall be a matter of doubt as to the position you may hold in regard to this most vital interest. Should the day ever come (and may it never come) when that persecuted spirit shall be banished from our older institutions, or what is scarcely better, enjoy only a formal recognition, God grant that hither it may take its flight, and here find its welcome and its home.

Brethren I have done. That the Great Head of the church may speed you in your work, is my earnest prayer; and having done your best till you can do no more, may he greet you with the plaudit, *"Well done,"* and say, *"Enter ye into the joy of your Lord."*